Samuel French Acting Edition

I0591722

Love, Noël
The Songs and Letters of Noël Coward

An entertainment devised by
Barry Day

SAMUELFRENCH.COM   SAMUELFRENCH.CO.UK

FOR PRODUCTION ENQUIRIES

UNITED STATES AND CANADA
Info@SamuelFrench.com
1-866-598-8449

UNITED KINGDOM AND EUROPE
Plays@SamuelFrench.co.uk
020-7255-4302

Each title is subject to availability from Samuel French, depending upon country of performance. Please be aware that *LOVE, NOËL* may not be licensed by Samuel French in your territory. Professional and amateur producers should contact the nearest Samuel French office or licensing partner to verify availability.

MUSIC USE NOTE

Licensees are solely responsible for obtaining formal written permission from copyright owners to use copyrighted music in the performance of this play and are strongly cautioned to do so. If no such permission is obtained by the licensee, then the licensee must use only original music that the licensee owns and controls. Licensees are solely responsible and liable for all music clearances and shall indemnify the copyright owners of the play(s) and their licensing agent, Samuel French, against any costs, expenses, losses and liabilities arising from the use of music by licensees. Please contact the appropriate music licensing authority in your territory for the rights to any incidental music.

IMPORTANT BILLING AND CREDIT REQUIREMENTS

If you have obtained performance rights to this title, please refer to your licensing agreement for important billing and credit requirements.

MUSIC COPYRIGHT

CHARACTERS

A **MAN** plays the following roles:

NOËL

YOUNG NOËL

ELYOT

A **WOMAN** plays the following roles:

COWARD'S MOTHER

MANON

ESMÉ

GEORGE BERNARD SHAW

GERTIE

AMANDA

DAPHNE

MARY MARTIN

BEA

ELAINE STRITCH

MARLENE

GARBO

ACTRESS

CLEMENCE DANE

LYNN

WOOLF

SITWELL

FERBER

BENITA

QUEEN MUM

AUTHOR'S NOTES

I would prefer the piece to be played straight through. However, if a management insists on an Intermission, I have indicated where this should be.

SONG LIST

(Pianist enters and goes to piano.)

(He begins to play **"SOMEDAY I'LL FIND YOU"** *from the beginning of the refrain.)*

*(***MAN*** and* **WOMAN** *enter and take their seats.)*

WOMAN. "Extraordinary how potent cheap music can be." Didn't Noël say something to that effect?

MAN. He said *exactly that* – and to exactly that piece of music. He also said that he'd always taken light music seriously.

It told you where you were when you first heard it...

WOMAN. ...And who you were with and how you felt...

MAN. Yes, in a way it defined you.

WOMAN. And, if I may say, he *might* have added that "they don't write them like they used to,"

MAN. Only too true, I'm afraid...

(They sing the first and second refrain of **"WHERE ARE THE SONGS WE SUNG?"***)*

GERTIE.

WHERE ARE THE SONGS WE SUNG
WHEN LOVE IN OUR HEARTS WAS YOUNG?
WHERE, IN THE LIMBO OF THE SWIFTLY PASSING YEARS,
LIE ALL OUR HOPES AND DREAMS AND FEARS?
WHERE HAVE THEY GONE – WORDS THAT RANG SO TRUE
WHEN LOVE IN OUR HEARTS WAS NEW?
WHERE IN THE SHADOWS THAT WE HAVE TO PASS AMONG
LIE THOSE SONGS THAT ONCE WE SUNG?

NOËL.

WHERE ARE THE SONGS WE SUNG
WHEN LOVE IN OUR HEARTS WAS YOUNG?
CAN YOU REMEMBER ALL THE FOOLISH THINGS WE SAID,
THE PLANS WE PLANNED – THE TEARS WE SHED?

WHERE IS IT NOW – THAT ENCHANTED DAWN
WHEN LOVE IN OUR HEARTS WAS BORN?

BOTH.

WHERE IN THE SHADOWS THAT WE HAVE TO PASS AMONG
LIE THOSE SONGS THAT ONCE WE SUNG?

> *(They now cease to be* **NOËL** *and* **GERTIE** *and become presenters…)*

WOMAN. If I had to pick a song that seemed to sum Noël up, it would be the one sung by Manon, the café chanteuse in *Bitter Sweet.*

> *(She sings the first verse and the refrain of* **"IF LOVE WERE ALL."***)*

LIFE IS VERY ROUGH AND TUMBLE
FOR A HUMBLE
DISEUSE;
ONE CAN BETRAY ONE'S TROUBLES NEVER,
WHATEVER
OCCURS,
NIGHT AFTER NIGHT,
HAVE TO LOOK BRIGHT,
WHETHER YOU'RE WELL OR ILL;
PEOPLE MUST LAUGH THEIR FILL.
YOU MUSTN'T SLEEP
TILL DAWN COMES CREEPING.
THOUGH I NEVER REALLY GRUMBLE
LIFE'S A JUMBLE
INDEED –
AND IN MY EFFORTS TO SUCCEED
I'VE HAD TO FORMULATE A CREED –

I BELIEVE IN DOING WHAT I CAN,
IN CRYING WHEN I MUST,
IN LAUGHING WHEN I CHOOSE.
HEIGH-O, IF LOVE WERE ALL
I SHOULD BE LONELY.
I BELIEVE THE MORE YOU LOVE A MAN,
THE MORE YOU GIVE YOUR TRUST,
THE MORE YOU'RE BOUND TO LOSE.

ALTHOUGH WHEN SHADOWS FALL
I THINK IF ONLY –
SOMEBODY SPLENDID REALLY NEEDED ME,
SOMEONE AFFECTIONATE AND DEAR,
CARES WOULD BE ENDED IF I KNEW THAT HE
WANTED TO HAVE ME NEAR.
BUT I BELIEVE THAT SINCE MY LIFE BEGAN
THE MOST I'VE HAD IS JUST
A TALENT TO AMUSE.
HEIGH-O, IF LOVE WERE ALL!

MAN. A "talent to amuse"?

Yes, but so much more. Remember the speech his friend Lord Louis Mountbatten gave at a party to celebrate Noël's 70th birthday?

WOMAN. "There are probably greater painters than Noël, greater novelists than Noël, greater librettists, greater composers of music, greater singers, greater dancers, greater comedians, greater tragedians, greater stage producers, greater film directors, greater cabaret artists, greater TV stars, and so on. If there are, they are fourteen different people. Only *one* man combined all fourteen different talents – The Master. Noël Coward."

MAN. And I don't think anyone has ever made a better summary of the man who bestrode the first three-quarters of the last century. Who did everything and knew everyone – as his letters testify. A Renaissance man who just happened to live in the twentieth century. More than anything else he wrote, his letters demonstrate his hopes, his fears and his friendships. And unlike his *Diaries*, they weren't written with an eye to eventual publication. They are precisely what he *felt* when he *wrote*. His literary DNA.

WOMAN. Many of his most important relationships were with women. There was his mother, Violet. He wrote to her every week when they were apart and – thank Heaven – she kept every one of his letters.

MAN. Fifty years of love – mingled with a good degree of mutual irritation. She was the archetypal "theatrical mothe," who lived through her son…

COWARD'S MOTHER. There is so much I could tell you of his dear ways and loving affection when he was a boy. No mother ever had such a son and I always feel that I am really and truly more proud of his love for me than of his great success.

MAN. Though she didn't mind his "great success"!

YOUNG NOËL. "Darling Mummy. Thank you for your nice long letter. I am sorry I did not write before, but I have got such a lot to do. You know I always want you just a very little bit at night when I go to bed and I generally cry a bit but it is nothing to speak of! Are there two vests of mine at home? It seems to me that I have been wearing the two that I have on now for ages. I think they are getting somewhat congealed. Please send me the other two."

COWARD'S MOTHER. And even when he was on holiday, he was still acting…

YOUNG NOËL. "I am having a fine time and I have had some real adventures. Yesterday I dressed up as an Arab and two very jolly girls dressed up in beads and hangings and we went through the village throwing flowers at everyone and telling their fortunes. It was fun."

NOËL. It wasn't quite so much fun a year or two later when I decided to dress up as a girl for one dinner party to see how long I could carry off the deception. It was perhaps a little too successful. A young man declared his passion in the garden and I had to steer him briskly indoors to the safety of the crowd. The next day a letter arrived at the house where I was staying…

"Dear Little Flapper, You can imagine my feelings when I arrived this morning to find that you had flown. I was fearfully sick, as I had been looking forward to spending an exceedingly pleasant morning with you. I do call it real hard lines and I am still feeling beastly depressed…

I have got a little remembrance of you, which I am
loath to part with – your cigarette holder. Should I be
presuming too much if I asked for your photo?"

He never did get the photo – and I never got my
cigarette holder.

Strangely "Dear Little Flapper" was never heard from
again.

WOMAN. There was his fellow juvenile actor, Esmé Wynne,
who was determined to be a writer and whose literary
obsession with fey little fairies – the ones that live at the
bottom of gardens – led Noël to want to compete and
write himself.

MAN. Esmé always felt she could pinpoint the precise
moment when his ambition to be a writer was fixed.

ESMÉ. It was during the engagement of *Where the Rainbow
Ends* at the Savoy Theatre, where we first met. I was the
leading lady and I was asked to write a three-act fairy
play for a special matinee. It got a great deal of extra
publicity because the censor banned it, on account of
its length.

All this excitement and publicity, so dear, even then, to
the heart of the youthful Noël, determined him to write
himself, and he suggested that we collaborate, as we did
in excruciatingly bad sketches, stories and songs during
the next few years.

NOËL. And, like all young actors of our generation, we
toured the provinces.

(They sing "TOURING DAYS.")

ESMÉ.

TOURING DAYS, TOURING DAYS,
WHATEVER IT SEEMS TO BE

NOËL.

SINCE THE LANDLADY AT NORWICH
SERVED A MOUSE UP IN THE PORRIDGE

ESMÉ.

AND A BEETLE IN THE MORNING TEA

BOTH.

> TOURING DAYS, ALLURING DAYS
> FAR BACK INTO THE PAST WE GAZE

NOËL.

> WE USED TO TIP THE DRESSERS EVERY FRIDAY NIGHT

ESMÉ.

> AND PASS IT OVER LIGHTLY WHEN THEY CAME IN TIGHT.

BOTH.

> BUT SOMEHOW TO US IT SEEMED ALL RIGHT,
> THOSE WONDERFUL TOURING DAYS.

WOMAN. But, of course, the whole *point* of touring the provinces was that someone important would spot your blazing talent and offer you a job in the West End...so that you wouldn't HAVE to tour the provinces.

YOUNG NOËL. Manchester. "My Darling Mummy, at the moment I am nearly mad with excitement. My dear, I am collaborating with Max Darewski on a song – he owns three theaters! I wrote the lyrics yesterday after breakfast, I hummed it to him in the Midland Hotel Lounge at twelve o'clock, and we at once rushed up to his private room and he put harmonies to it. Max leaped off the piano stool and danced for joy and said it was going to take London by storm. It is called 'When You Come Home on Leave.'"

WOMAN. Well, of course, it *didn't* take London by storm. Ivor Novello's "Keep the Home Fires Burning" did that. But one thing did lead to another...and quite quickly, too.

YOUNG NOËL. "Darling Mummy, I was sent for to see Gilbert Miller (the great American impresario). He had come down especially to see me and he said I was really splendid in the play. He wants me for a terrific part in *The Saving Grace* with Sir Charles Hawtrey. Isn't it gorgeous?! He says he has perfect confidence in me and that I am thoroughly natural and unaffected. Oh, I am a star!"

WOMAN. Well, not exactly a *star*. But it was a start. He could never be accused of not aiming high. One of his early plays was *The Young Idea.*

NOËL. ...Based, I'm afraid, all too closely, on Bernard Shaw's *You Can Never Tell.* Well, Shaw *could* tell and when I sent him the script... He returned it with detailed annotations, such as "No, you don't young Author!" and a little note which read...

GEORGE BERNARD SHAW. "I have no doubt you will succeed if you persevere and take care, above all, never to see or read my plays. Unless you can get clean and away from me, you will begin as a back number, and be hopelessly out of it when you are forty."

MAN. Not exactly encouraging.

WOMAN. – but more than compensated for by a message from Gilbert Miller, which he could not wait to convey to Violet.

NOËL. My play *The Last Trick* accepted for America. Stop. Advance of five hundred dollars. Stop. Passing peacefully away. Stop. Love Noël.

WOMAN. America – here he came In June of 1921...

NOËL. I felt that some sort of scene was necessary to celebrate my first entrance into America, so I said – "Little Lamb, who made thee?" – to a customs official... A fracas far exceeding my wildest dreams ensued, during which he delved down with malice aforethought to the bottom of a trunk and discovered the oddest things in my sponge bag. I think I am going to like America.

WOMAN. One of the things – in fact, *two* of the things – he liked best were Lynn Fontanne and Alfred Lunt...living together in extremely close proximity but not yet "The Lunts" ...He wrote to Violet:

NOËL. "Darling. Do you remember Lynn Fontanne? She played some small parts in London and came to New York. Well, she's had a huge success in a play called *Dulcy,* (she's Dulcy). I went to see her opening night with her fiancé, an actor called Alfred Lunt and, my dear, a star was born. Well, two stars, actually, as Alfred is also making a name for himself in these parts. They're quite wonderful and couldn't have been kinder to me. They haven't any money either – though they soon will have, I'm sure – and they helped me keep body and soul together by sharing their last crust (not quite that, really!) They're going to be huge stars and, since we all know that yours truly is going to be one too, we've decided that when that great day arrives, we shall act together in a play I shall write for us and the cosmos will have a new galaxy. Well, that's all for now. Must rush or the Astors and Vanderbilts will think I'm not coming. Won't be long now before your dear son is back to bore everyone with his stories and exploits, some of which actually happened."

WOMAN. His verdict on that first visit to New York?

NOËL. It seemed, in spite of its hardness and irritating, noisy efficiency, a great and exciting place...

> *(**NOËL** sings the first refrain of "I LIKE AMERICA.")*

I LIKE AMERICA,
I HAVE PLAYED AROUND EV'RY
SLAPPY-HAPPY HUNTING GROUND
BUT I FIND AMERICA – OKAY.
I'VE BEEN ABOUT A BIT
BUT I MUST ADMIT
THAT I DIDN'T KNOW THE HALF OF IT
TILL I HIT THE U.S.A.
NO LIKELY LASS
IN BOSTON, MASS.
FROM PASSION WILL RECOIL.
IN DALLAS, TEX.
THEY TALK OF SEX
BUT ONLY THINK OF OIL.
NEW JERSEY DAMES
GO UP IN FLAMES
IF SOMEONE MENTIONS "BED."
IN CHICAGO, ILLINOIS

ANY GIRL WHO MEETS A BOY
GIGGLES AND SHOOTS HIM DEAD!
BUT I LIKE AMERICA
ITS SOCIETY
OFFERS INFINITE VARIETY
AND COME WHAT MAY
I SHALL RETURN SOME DAY
TO THE GOOD OLD U.S.A.
HEY, HEY.
HEY, HEY.

WOMAN. And return he did – many times. It became a second home. And the Lunts, a second family. They would be one of the threads throughout the rest of his life. Another would be Gertrude Alexandra Dagmar Lawrence-Klausen... *Gertie.*

(MAN) NOËL. I first met her as yet another child actor... She was a vivacious child with ringlets to whom I took an instant fancy. She was very mondaine, carried a handbag with a powder puff and frequently dabbed her generously turned-up nose. She then gave me an orange and told me a few mildly dirty stories, and I loved her from then onwards.

GERTIE. I think it's pretty clear the attraction was mutual.

> (**GERTIE** *sings the first refrain of* **"MAD ABOUT THE BOY."**)

MAD ABOUT THE BOY,
I KNOW IT'S STUPID TO BE MAD ABOUT THE BOY,
I'M SO ASHAMED OF IT, BUT MUST ADMIT
THE SLEEPLESS NIGHTS I'VE HAD ABOUT THE BOY.
ON THE SILVER SCREEN
HE MELTS MY FOOLISH HEART IN EV'RY SINGLE SCENE,
ALTHOUGH I'M QUITE AWARE THAT HERE AND THERE
ARE TRACES OF THE CAD ABOUT THE BOY.
LORD KNOWS I'M NOT A FOOL GIRL,
I REALLY SHOULDN'T CARE.
LORD KNOWS I'M NOT A SCHOOLGIRL
IN THE FLURRY OF HER FIRST AFFAIR.
WILL IT EVER CLOY?

THIS ODD DIVERSITY OF MISERY AND JOY;
I'M FEELING QUITE INSANE AND YOUNG AGAIN,
AND ALL BECAUSE I'M MAD ABOUT THE BOY.

NOËL. In 1929 Gertie appeared in a straight play, *Candle-Light*, which drew one of my pithy cables... "Legitimate at last, won't Mother be pleased?"

A few months later, I had written *Private Lives* as a vehicle for the two of us. As soon as I put my pen down, I cabled... "I Have Written Delightful New Comedy. Stop. Good Part For You. Stop. Wonderful One For Me. Stop. Keep Yourself Free For Autumn Production."

GERTIE. "Have Read New Play. Stop. Nothing Wrong That Can't Be Fixed. Stop. Gertie."

NOËL. "The Only Thing That Will Need To Be Fixed Is Your Performance. Stop. Noël."

When the sheer weight and the expense of the cables got too much, I finally received a *letter* from the lady, who was holidaying in the South of France.

GERTIE. "Darling! Am I wrong or did I hear you mention something about a play we were going to do in London first and then in America? Please let me know, because me 'ouse is as full as a pig and I would like to do something about putting up with you – sorry – I mean – well, you know – should you wish to visit me here to discuss ways and means. Love, Gert."

NOËL. "With regard to the illiterate scrawl of 14th inst., Mr. Coward asks me to say that there was talk of your playing a small part in a play of his on condition that you tour and find your own clothes (of reasonable quality) and understudy Jessie Matthews, whom you have always imitated. Mr. Coward will appear, whether you like it or not, on the 20th..."

"If by chance there is no room in the rather squalid lodgings you have taken, would you be so kind as to engage several suites for Mr. C. which will enable him to have every conceivable meal with you and use all your toilets for his own advantage... The terms you agreed upon- i.e., six pounds, two shillings a week and understudy…"

And of course we did do *Private Lives* – and became "Noël & Gertie" overnight and forever after.

*(Piano plays strains from **"SOMEDAY I'LL FIND YOU."**)*

AMANDA. Nasty insistent little tune.

ELYOT. Yes, isn't it? Strange how potent cheap music is.

AMANDA. What have you been doing lately? During these last years?

ELYOT. Travelling about. I went round the world you know after –

AMANDA. Yes, yes, I know. How was it?

ELYOT. The world?

AMANDA. Yes.

ELYOT. Oh, highly enjoyable.

AMANDA. China must be very interesting.

ELYOT. Very big, China.

AMANDA. And Japan –

ELYOT. Very small.

AMANDA. Did you eat sharks' fins, and take your shoes off, and use chopsticks and everything?

ELYOT. Practically everything.

AMANDA. And India, the burning Ghars, or Ghats or whatever they are, and the Taj Mahal. How was the Taj Mahal?

ELYOT. *(Looking at her.)* Unbelievable, a sort of dream.

AMANDA. That was the moonlight, I expect, you must have seen it in the moonlight.

ELYOT. *(Not taking his eyes off her.)* Yes, moonlight is cruelly deceptive.

AMANDA. And it didn't look like a biscuit box did it? I've always felt that it might.

ELYOT. Darling, darling, I love you so.

(**AMANDA** *sings the first verse and the refrain of*
"SOMEDAY I'LL FIND YOU.")

AMANDA.

WHEN ONE IS LONELY THE DAYS ARE LONG;
YOU SEEM SO NEAR
BUT NEVER APPEAR.
EACH NIGHT I SING YOU A LOVER'S SONG;
PLEASE TRY, TRY TO HEAR,
MY DEAR, MY DEAR.

SOMEDAY I'LL FIND YOU,
MOONLIGHT BEHIND YOU,
TRUE TO THE DREAM I AM DREAMING.
AS I DRAW NEAR YOU
YOU'LL SMILE A LITTLE SMILE;
FOR A LITTLE WHILE
WE SHALL STAND
HAND IN HAND.
I'LL LEAVE YOU NEVER,
LOVE YOU FOREVER,
ALL OUR PAST SORROW REDEEMING:
MAKE IT ALL COME TRUE,
MAKE ME LOVE YOU, TOO,
SOMEDAY I'LL FIND YOU AGAIN.

ELYOT. You always had a sweet voice, Amanda.

AMANDA. *(Huskily, with emotion.)* Thank you.

MAN. When *Cavalcade* opened on October 13, 1931 at the Theatre Royal, Drury Lane, Gertie was in the first night audience.

GERTIE. "Here I am down on my knees to you in humble admiration and complete adoration. I didn't wire you last night, because I felt too near you to mix my stupid pence worth of good wishes with those many who couldn't have been feeling as deeply as I was; but please believe me when I tell you that I spent the whole evening from eight till eleven with my hand tightly clasped in yours – anything just to feel that I might perhaps be some subconscious support to you. As you say, it's 'pretty exciting to be English.' But also it's pretty exciting to love you as I do. This, you may be surprised to see, is from 'Ole Gert.'"

NOËL. There was a general impression that Gertie and I played together continuously. In fact, we were only together in three productions – *Tonight At 8:30* was the third and last.

GERTIE. And for me – the best…

> *(They sing the first verse and the refrain of* **"YOU WERE THERE."***)*

GERTIE.

WAS IT IN THE REAL WORLD?
OR WAS IT IN A DREAM?
WAS IT JUST A NOTE FROM SOME ETERNAL THEME?

NOËL.

WAS IT ACCIDENTAL
OR ACCURATELY PLANNED?
HOW COULD I HESITATE
KNOWING THAT MY FATE
LED ME BY THE HAND?

GERTIE.

YOU WERE THERE,
I SAW YOU AND MY HEART STOPPED BEATING.

NOËL.

YOU WERE THERE,
AND IN THAT FIRST ENCHANTED MEETING
LIFE CHANGED ITS TUNE,
THE STARS, THE MOON
CAME NEAR TO ME.

GERTIE.

DREAMS THAT I DREAMED
LIKE MAGIC SEEMED
TO BE CLEAR TO ME, DEAR TO ME.

BOTH.
> YOU WERE THERE,
> YOUR EYES LOOKED INTO MINE AND FALTERED.
> EVERYWHERE
> THE COLOR OF THE WHOLE WORLD ALTERED.
> FALSE BECAME TRUE,
> MY UNIVERSE TUMBLED IN TWO,
> THE EARTH BECAME HEAVEN, FOR YOU
> WERE THERE.

NOËL. We planned a number of other projects but somehow they never came to anything.

Even though Gertie would write...

GERTIE. "I would so much like us to be back once more hand in hand at curtain calls."

NOËL. And, in any case, Gertie had a number of other successes of her own, such as the Kurt Weill/Ira Gershwin musical, *Lady in the Dark*, in 1941. I'm afraid I couldn't resist a cable... "Hope you get a warm hand on your opening."

"You were there." She'd *always* be there for me.

Until...one day – she *wasn't*...

Perhaps her biggest personal success in later years was *The King and I*, which Rodgers & Hammerstein had written specially for her. It opened in 1951 and won every award one had ever heard of – and quite a few one hadn't. But there were problems here – and they surfaced quite suddenly...

They were to do with Gertie's voice – never strong but now becoming decidedly problematic, even through Richard Rodgers had composed the songs specially for her vocal range. Then there seemed to be a remission.

GERTIE. "Well, wadderyerknow? After that short siege of vocal doldrums my voice suddenly returned, my spirits rose and my hackles fairly bristled with vitality. So it seems there is not too much to worry about – I just struck a bad patch and you came and sat in it!

Oh dear – and it's always you I want to please above *anyone.*"

NOËL. But it wasn't just a bad patch. I only learned later that her condition worsened again and this time dramatically.

The doctors appeared to be baffled and the only ones who knew the gravity of the situation were her agent, Fanny Holtzmann and her sometime lover, Daphne Du Maurier. I read about her death in the evening paper, of all things!

Poor, darling old Gertie – a lifelong friend. With all her overacting and silliness, I never knew her do a mean or unkind thing. I am terribly unhappy to think that I shall never see her again.

Later Daphne wrote to me…

DAPHNE. I was pretty sure something was wrong and had been for some time. That real exhaustion to do anything every Sunday but just lie on the chaise-longue, turban on her head, Nivea skin oil on her face, plaid rug over the knees, steam heat at full blast, enough to kill anyone, Angus the Scottie lying panting at her feet. I remember creeping in to see if she wanted anything and kissing her silly cock-eyed nose, and she opened one eye and said – "I thought it was Angus." – "It was," I said and went…

Why, oh why, should someone with the mind of somebody of ten – with whom one really had no thought in common, no topic of real conversation, no sort of outlook resembling one's own at all, who frequently lied, who never stopped doing the most infuriating things – have the power to so completely wrap herself around the heart that, because of her, one became bitched, buggered and bewildered?

The night before I left – and it will be my last memory of her – she had the eternal radio switched on, it went on through the night, and suddenly your *Bitter Sweet* song came over, the "I'll See You Again" song, and she began to sing it, from her pillow, in that lilting, sexless, choir-boy voice that was her true voice, very softly, and I told her *that* was what I meant, to sing always like that, but she said I was being sentimental, and rushed off to some new teacher who was to make her sing like Patti, Melba, Flagstad, the works.

NOËL. I met Daphne again at a party some years later and she told me how Gertie had always regretted that she never had the opportunity to sing "I'll See You Again" – even though I had originally written it for her…

> (**GERTIE** *sings the refrain of* **"I'LL SEE YOU AGAIN."**)

GERTIE.

> I'LL SEE YOU AGAIN
> WHENEVER SPRING BREAKS THROUGH AGAIN.
> TIME MAY LIE HEAVY BETWEEN,
> BUT WHAT HAS BEEN
> IS PAST FORGETTING.

> YOUR SWEET MEMORY
> ACROSS THE YEARS WILL COME TO ME.
> THOUGH MY WORLD MAY GO AWRY,
> IN MY HEART WILL EVER LIE,
> JUST THE ECHO OF A SIGH,
> GOODBYE.

NOËL. Sometimes I would look across the stage at her – and she would take my breath away.

> (**NOËL** *sings, unaccompanied – almost as an echo.*)

> THOUGH MY WORLD MAY GO AWRY,
> AND I NEVER SAID GOODBYE,
> I SHALL LOVE YOU TILL I DIE…

> (*He finds it impossible to say the final "Goodbye" and looks away.*)

GERTIE. Goodbye

> (**NOËL** *sings the refrain of* **"I'LL REMEMBER HER."**)

NOËL.

> I'LL REMEMBER HER,
> HOW INCREDIBLY NAIVE SHE WAS,
> I COULDN'T QUITE BELIEVE SHE WAS SINCERE.
> SO ALERT, SO IMPERTINENT, AND YET SO SWEET.
> MY DEFEAT WAS CLEAR.
> I'LL REMEMBER HER,
> HER ABSURD EXAGGERATING
> AND HER UTTERLY DEFLATING REPARTEE
> AND THE ONLY THING THAT WORRIES ME AT ALL
> IS WHETHER SHE'LL REMEMBER ME.
>
> I'LL REMEMBER HER
> IN THE EVENINGS WHEN I'M LONELY
> AND IMAGINING IF ONLY
> SHE WERE THERE.
> I'LL RELIVE, OH, SO VIVIDLY, OUR SAD AND SWEET,
> INCOMPLETE AFFAIR.
>
> I'LL REMEMBER HER
> HEAVY-HEARTED WHEN WE PARTED.
> WITH HER EYES SO FULL OF TEARS SHE COULDN'T SEE
> AND I'LL FEEL INSIDE A FOOLISH SORT OF PRIDE
> TO THINK THAT SHE REMEMBERS ME.

NOËL. It's more than likely that Gertie spoiled me for other leading ladies – and there were many of those... I remember once saying – "God preserve me in future from female stars. I don't suppose He will." And, indeed, He didn't...

There were some – like Yvonne Printemps – who couldn't help it. In *Conversation Piece* I remember her English was negligible throughout but by the end of the run the whole company was speaking excellent French! At one point she delivered the immortal line- "The clouds are pissing over the sun." Well, there really is no answer to that.

There was Mary Martin in *Pacific 1860*. On one occasion I had to point out to her that one does not say to Princess Margaret –

MARY MARTIN. "Give my best to your sister. Bye-bye for now."

NOËL. However, a few years later we were "together with music" again and very happily so – so that was all right.

> *(They sing part of the first refrain and move into the second refrain of "TOGETHER WITH MUSIC.")*

BOTH.

TOGETHER WITH MUSIC,
TOGETHER WITH MUSIC,
WE PLANNED THIS MOMENT LONG AGO.

MARY MARTIN.

MANY A YEAR WE'VE SIGHED IN VAIN
FOR BOTH OF US KNEW

NOËL.

MANY A MOON WOULD WAX AND WANE
BEFORE THIS DREAM CAME TRUE

BOTH.

TOGETHER WITH MUSIC,
TOGETHER WITH MUSIC,

> *(Jump to second rerfrain's lyrics.)*

AT LAST THE GODS HAVE SAID OKAY

MARY MARTIN.

WHEN THOSE FIRST NOTES WE HEAR,
A MILLION STARS APPEAR

NOËL.

OUR PERSONAL WORLD GOES ROUND AND ROUND,

MARY MARTIN.

GAILY WIRED FOR SOUND.

BOTH.

EV'RYTHING'S SHINING AND BRIGHT.
THIS IS OUR JUBILEE,
BECAUSE AT LONG, LONG LAST WE HAPPEN TO BE
TOGETHER WITH MUSIC TONIGHT.

NOËL. *After The Ball.* Mea culpa there, I'm afraid. Physically the years had treated her kindly but, sadly, not her voice – which *was* rather the point of the show.

But at least Miss Ellis knew the words. Someone who never did and would drive me absolutely mad was my darling Bea Lillie. There have been times when I have been so frustrated by the way Beattie mangled my lines that I had to retire to the lobby and jump up and down. In the beginning – before I knew better – I tried *everything.* On one occasion, when she was coming to New York by ship to appear in a revue of mine, I resorted to cabling her and even using her title, Lady Peel...

"Pretty Witty Lady Peel
Never Mind How Sick You Feel
Never Mind Your Broken Heart
Concentrate and Learn Your Part!"

And what did I get back?

BEA.
"Thanks Musty Dusty Noël C
For Beastly Wire to Lady P
To Concentrate is Hard I Fear
So Now She's Crying in her Beer."

NOËL. But what she does do instead of what one writes for her has a certain beguiling magic and audiences love her. Now *that* is star quality.

WOMAN. It was a quality he immediately recognized in Elaine Stritch. He also recognized that in dealing with her the velvet glove had better contain an iron – if ironic – fist.

NOËL. "Darling Stritchie,
I hope that you are well, that your cold is better, that you are singing divinely, that you are putting on weight, that you are not belting too much, that your skin is clear and free from spots and other blemishes, that you are delivering my brilliant material to the public in the

manner in which it should be delivered, that you are not making too many Goddamned suggestions, that your breath is relatively free from the sinful taint of alcohol, that you are going regularly to confession and everywhere else that is necessary to go regularly.

NOËL. *(cont.)* I also hope that you are not encouraging those dear little doggies to behave in such a fashion on the stage that they bring disrepute to the fair name of Equity and add fuel to the already prevalent suspicion that our gallant little company is not, by and large, entirely normal. I also hope that you are not constantly taking those silly Walter Kerr and Agnes G. de Mille to the Pavilion for lunch every day… They only exhaust you and drain your energy and, however much you want to keep in with them, you must remember that your first duty is to me and the Catholic Church – in that order.

I remain yours sincerely with mad hot kisses."

ELAINE STRITCH. "Now Noël, are you sitting down – ready? I don't drink at all – anything – I mean anything, any more and I must say it's an adventure. The results have been world shaking. I look and feel about thirteen years old. I'm up at ten, do my own marketing, walk the dog three times a day in the park. I've been to the laundromat! One of the biggest decisions in life of late is whether or not it will be V8 juice, plain tonic (sugar-free) or unsweetened grapefruit at cocktail time.

You have a strange effect on me – every time I see you and talk to you, I somehow immediately go on the wagon. So what does that mean?

(Unless, of course, I'm working for you in which case I double my intake.)

I've had two beers a day since I saw you last. Well, *three* today."

NOËL. Two beers or three – Stritchie could certainly put a number across.

(**WOMAN** *sings three refrains of* ***"WHY DO THE WRONG PEOPLE TRAVEL?"***)

WOMAN.

WHY DO THE WRONG PEOPLE TRAVEL, TRAVEL, TRAVEL,
WHEN THE RIGHT PEOPLE STAY BACK HOME?
WHAT COMPULSION COMPELS THEM
AND WHO THE HELL TELLS THEM
TO DRAG THEIR BAGS TO ZANZIBAR,
INSTEAD OF STAYING QUIETLY IN OMAHA?
THE TAJ MAHAL
AND THE GRAND CANAL
AND THE SUNNY FRENCH RIVIERA
WOULD BE LESS OPPRESSED
IF THE MIDDLE WEST
WOULD SETTLE FOR SOMEWHERE RATHER NEARER.
PLEASE DO NOT THINK THAT I CRITICIZE OR CAVIL
AT A GENUINE URGE TO ROAM
BUT WHY, OH WHY, DO THE WRONG PEOPLE TRAVEL
WHEN THE RIGHT PEOPLE STAY BACK HOME,
AND MIND THEIR BUS'NESS
WHEN THE RIGHT PEOPLE STAY BACK HOME
WITH TELEVISION,
WHEN THE RIGHT PEOPLE STAY BACK HOME
I'M MERELY ASKING
WHY THE RIGHT PEOPLE STAY BACK HOME?

WHY DO THE WRONG PEOPLE TRAVEL, TRAVEL, TRAVEL,
WHEN THE RIGHT PEOPLE STAY BACK HOME?
WHAT EXPLAINS THIS MASS MANIA
TO LEAVE PENNSYLVANIA
AND CLACK AROUND LIKE FLOCKS OF GEESE,
DEMANDING DRY MARTINIS ON THE ISLES OF GREECE?
IN THE SMALLEST STREET,
WHERE THE GOURMETS MEET,
THEY INVARIABLY FETCH UP
AND IT'S HARD TO MAKE THEM ACCEPT A STEAK
THAT ISN'T SERVED RARE AND SMEARED WITH KETCHUP.
IT WOULD TAKE YEARS TO UNRAVEL, RAVEL, RAVEL

EV'RY IMPULSE THAT MAKES THEM ROAM.
BUT WHY, OH WHY DO THE WRONG PEOPLE TRAVEL
WHEN THE RIGHT PEOPLE STAY BACK HOME
AND EAT DOUGHNUTS,
WHEN THE RIGHT PEOPLE STAY BACK HOME
WITH ALL THAT LETTUCE,
WHEN THE RIGHT PEOPLE STAY BACK HOME
I SOMETIMES WONDER
WHY THE RIGHT PEOPLE STAY BACK HOME.

WOMAN. *(cont.)*

WHY DO THE WRONG PEOPLE TRAVEL, TRAVEL, TRAVEL,
WHEN THE RIGHT PEOPLE STAY BACK HOME?
WHAT PECULIAR OBSESSIONS
INSPIRE THOSE PROCESSIONS
OF FAMILIES FROM HOUSTON, TEX.
WITH ALL THOSE CAMERAS AROUNDS THEIR NECKS?
THEY WILL TAKE A TRAIN OR AN AEROPLANE
FOR AN HOUR ON THE COSTA BRAVA
AND THEY'LL SEE POMPEII ON THE ONLY DAY
THAT IT'S UP TO ITS EARS IN MOLTON LAVA.
MILLIONS OF TOURISTS ARE CHURNING UP THE GRAVEL
WHILE THEY GAZE AT ST. PETER'S DOME,
BUT WHY OH WHY DO THE WRONG PEOPLE TRAVEL
WHEN THE RIGHT PEOPLE STAY BACK HOME?
AND PLAY CANASTA
WHEN THE RIGHT PEOPLE STAY BACK HOME.
WON'T SOMEONE TELL ME
WHY THE RIGHT PEOPLE STAY BACK HOME?

NOËL. And then, of course, there was our legendary, lovely, Marlene. She phones me from Hollywood after she'd seen my first real film, *The Scoundrel*, in 1935. I thought it was someone playing a practical joke, and hung up. But when Miss Dietrich cabled me the next day…

MARLENE. "I see you every night and talk of you all day. Stop. Marlene."

NOËL. Well, what's a boy to do…?

One of the things I did was to become her lifelong friend – and she mine. She would meet my ship or plane…

cook me the occasional meal, like the good German *hausfrau* she was under the glamorous façade…and wash everything in sight. On one occasion, including my hairbrush – which was already perfectly clean.

It was always my ambition to teach her about humor, as in "sense of humor." Unteachable, I suspect. I once said to her wittily that "all I required of my friends these days was that they should survive through lunch." She gave me a puzzled look…

MARLENE. Why lunch, sweetheart?

NOËL. There was a certain price to pay, I must admit. I had to hold her hand (metaphorically) through her many love affairs… Ed Murrow, Jean Gabin, Michael Wilding (twice – at least), Adlai Stevenson, Frank Sinatra, Kirk Douglas, Edith Piaf – how much time do you have? And Yul Brynner… Oh God, Yul Brynner…

MARLENE. "Last week in New York, I stood at the door when he came. I was not going to do one wrong thing. He came in smiling and told me about Paris, the fog around the Eiffel Tower, the streets, the bridges and how he thought about me…

I stood there thinking, this is not a dream. He is really back and he loves me. I made coffee as usual, gave him aspirin as usual after a drinking night. He left as usual a bit vague and at the door I said *as usual*, 'When will I hear from you?' and he said: 'Later.'

He did not call. Sinatra opened that night at the Copacabana. I went at midnight. He was there. I went home. He did not call. There was something wrong. I called him and I said, 'I want you to know there will be no complications again, no scenes, no trouble ever, no questions.' He said, 'Thank you, ma'am.' He said, 'How did you like Sinatra?' He saw me there and smiled to me very sweetly and intimately. I said, 'I thought it was terrible. Sinatra was drunk, had no voice, very unprofessional.' He said, 'I sat with him till eight in the morning.'

MARLENE. *(cont.)* Again I said, 'Can't you phone me later tonight?' He said: 'No.' I said, "What's wrong?" He said, 'I want nothing anymore. I have no confidence in anyone or anything anymore. Not in you either. You asked for it.' I phoned him later but the phone just rang – just that empty buzzing sound.

Noël, darling – I love you so very much and I long for you, not only out of loneliness or to throw my burden on you. I long so much for intelligence and brain food! Love, love, love, love to you, my exalted friend of the soul and the heart. And God bless you forever.
Marlene."

NOËL. I wrote to her from Jamaica... "Oh darling, your letter filled me with such a lot of emotions, the predominant one being rage that you should allow yourself to be so humiliated and made so unhappy by a situation that really isn't worthy of you. It is difficult for me to wag my finger at you from so far away, particularly as my heart aches for you but really, darling, you must pack up this nonsensical situation once and for all...

It is really beneath your dignity – not your dignity as a famous artist and a glamorous star, but your dignity as a human, only too human, being. Curly is attractive, beguiling, tender and fascinating, but he is not the only man in the world who merits those delightful adjectives.

To hell with God damned l'amour. It always causes far more trouble than it's worth. Don't run after it. Don't court it. Keep it waiting off stage until you're good and ready for it and even then treat it with the suspicious disdain that it deserves... I am sick to death of you waiting about in empty houses and apartments with your ears strained for the telephone to ring. Snap out of it, girl! A very brilliant writer once said (Could it have been me?), 'Life is for the living.' Well, that is all it is for, and living *does not* consist of staring in at other people's windows and waiting for crumbs to be thrown at you. You've carried on this hole in corner, overcharged, romantic, unrealistic nonsense long enough.

Stop it. Stop it. Other people need you… Incidentally, there is one fairly strong-minded type who will never let you down and who loves you very much indeed. Just try to guess who it is." How much good it did, I'll never know.

WOMAN. Falling in love again?

> *(She pauses in thought.)*

> *(She sings the refrain of "**NEVER AGAIN.**")*

NO, NEVER AGAIN,
NEVER THE STRANGE UNTHINKING JOY,
NEVER THE PAIN,
LET ME BE WISE,
LET ME LEARN TO DOUBT ROMANCE,
TRY TO LIVE WITHOUT ROMANCE,
LET ME BE SANE.
TIME CHANGES THE TUNE
CHANGES THE PALE UNWINKING STARS,
EVEN THE MOON.
LET ME BE SOON
STRONG ENOUGH TO FLOUT ROMANCE –
AND SAY, 'YOU'RE OUT, ROMANCE,'
NEVER AGAIN.

MAN. Love. Well…

> *(He sings the bridge from "**SAIL AWAY.**")*

LOVE IS MEANT TO MAKE YOU GLAD,
LOVE CAN MAKE THE WORLD GO ROUND,
LOVE CAN DRIVE YOU RAVING MAD,
TORMENT YOU AND UPSET YOU,
LOVE CAN GIVE YOUR HEART A JOLT
BUT PHILOSOPHERS HAVE FOUND
THAT IT'S WISE TO DO A BOLT
WHEN IT STARTS TO GET YOU DOWN…

WOMAN. So you're saying that "first fine careless rapture" doesn't last?

MAN. *I'm* not saying it. Robert Browning did. Sometimes it was never really there to begin with. And do you know the *worst* thing? By the time they realise it – Jack and Jill are Darby and Joan...

(They sing **"BRONXVILLE DARBY AND JOAN."**)

BOTH.

WE DO NOT FEAR THE VERDICT OF POSTERITY
OUR LIVES HAVE BEEN TOO HUMDRUM AND MUNDANE.

WOMAN.

IN THE TWILIGHT OF OUR DAYS

MAN.

HAVING REACHED THE FINAL PHASE

WOMAN.

IN ALL SINCERITY

MAN.

WE MUST EXPLAIN:

BOTH.

WE'RE A DEAR OLD COUPLE AND WE HATE ONE ANOTHER
AND WE'VE HATED ONE ANOTHER FOR A LONG, LONG
   TIME.

MAN.

SINCE THE DAY WE WERE WED, UP TO THE PRESENT,
OUR LIVES, WE MUST CONFESS
HAVE BEEN PROGRESSIVELY MORE UNPLEASANT.

BOTH.

WE'RE JUST SWEET OLD DARLINGS WHO DESPISE ONE
   ANOTHER
WITH A THOROUGHNESS APPROACHING THE SUBLIME,
BUT THROUGH ALL OUR YEARS
WE'VE BEEN AFFECTIONATELY KNOWN
AS THE BRONXVILLE DARBY AND JOAN.

MAN.

OUR GOLDEN WEDDING PASSED WITH ALL OUR FAMILY

WOMAN.

AN ORGY OF REMEMBRANCE AND RUE,

MAN.

IN ACKNOWLEDGEMENT OF THIS

WOMAN.

> WE EXCHANGED A LOVING KISS
> A TRIFLE CLAMMILY

BOTH.

> BECAUSE WE KNEW:
> WE'RE A DEAR OLD COUPLE WHO DETEST ONE ANOTHER,
> WE'VE DETESTED ONE ANOTHER SINCE OUR BRIDAL NIGHT,
> WHICH WAS SQUALID, UNATTRACTIVE AND CONVULSIVE
> AND PROVED, BEYOND DISPUTE,
> THAT WE WERE MUTUALLY REPULSIVE.
> WE'RE JUST SWEET OLD DARLINGS
> WHO TORMENT ONE ANOTHER
> WITH THE UTMOST MALICIOUSNESS AND SPITE,
> AND THROUGH ALL OUR YEARS
> WE'VE BEEN INACCURATELY KNOWN
> AS THE BRONXVILLE DARBY AND JOAN.

WOMAN. Do you know what I'd do if I felt that was happening to me?

MAN. I think I've a pretty good idea…

> (**MAN** *and* **WOMAN** *sing the refrain of* **"SAIL AWAY."**)

WOMAN.

> WHEN THE STORM CLOUDS ARE RIDING THROUGH A
>   WINTER SKY,
> SAIL AWAY – SAIL AWAY

MAN.

> WHEN THE LOVE-LIGHT IS FADING IN YOUR SWEETHEART'S
>   EYE,
> SAIL AWAY – SAIL AWAY

BOTH.

> WHEN YOU FEEL YOUR SONG IS ORCHESTRATED WRONG
> WHY SHOULD YOU PROLONG
> YOUR STAY?
> WHEN THE WIND AND THE WEATHER BLOW YOUR DREAMS
>   SKY HIGH,
> SAIL AWAY – SAIL AWAY – SAIL AWAY

[If the show is played with an intermission:]

MAN. I think we might 'sail away' ourselves for a few minutes.

WOMAN. I believe they call it an Intermission...

(*They exit.*)

[Intermission]

[The actors return.]

WOMAN. You had a lot of highlights in your career.
What were the *low* lights?

NOËL. I can tell you the *second* lowest...
You've finished the show. You've given your all and you
go out for a quiet drink with friends.
And then...
Somebody spots you...and comes over...

(**WOMAN** *acts "Social Grace."*)

I expect you've heard this a million times before
But I absolutely adored your last play
I went four times – and now to think
That I am actually talking to you!
It's thrilling! Honestly it is, I mean,
It's always thrilling, isn't it, to meet someone really celebrated?
I mean someone who really does things.
I expect all this is a terrible bore for you.
After all you go everywhere and know everybody.
It must be wonderful to go absolutely everywhere
And know absolutely everybody and – Oh dear –
Then to have to listen to someone like me,
I mean someone absolutely ordinary just one of your public.
No one will believe me when I tell them
That I have actually been talking to the great man himself.
It must be wonderful to be so frightfully brainy
And know all the things that you know.
I'm not brainy a bit, neither is my husband,
Just plain humdrum, that's what we are.
But we do come up to town occasionally
And go to shows and things. Actually my husband
Is quite a critic, not professionally, of course,
What I mean is that he isn't all that easily pleased.
He doesn't like everything. Oh no, not by any means.
He simply hated that thing at the Haymarket
Which everybody went on about. 'Rubbish,' he said
Straight out like that, 'Damned Rubbish!'
I nearly died because heaps of people were listening.

But that's quite typical of him. He just says what he thinks.
And he can't stand all this highbrow stuff –
Do you know what I mean? – All these plays about people being
    miserable
And never getting what they want and not even committing suicide
But just being absolutely wretched. He says he goes to the theatre
To have a good time. That's why he simply loves all your things.
I mean they relax him and he doesn't need to think.
And he certainly does love a good laugh.
You should have seen him the other night when we went to that film
With what's – her – name in it – I can't remember the title.
I thought he'd have a fit, honestly I did.
You must know the one I mean, the one about the man who comes
    home
And finds his wife has been carrying on with his best friend
And, of course, he's furious at first and then he decides to teach her
    a lesson.
You must have seen it. I wish I could remember the name
But that's absolutely typical of me, I've got a head like a sieve,
I keep on forgetting things and as for names – well!
I cannot for the life of me remember them.
Faces yes, I never forget a face because I happen to be naturally
    observant
And always have been since I was a tiny kiddie
But names – Oh dear! I'm quite hopeless.
I feel such a fool sometimes
I do honestly.

NOËL. As I say, that was the *second* lowest.

WOMAN. And the *lowest* lowest?

NOËL. When that *didn't* happen!

WOMAN. The thing I've never understood is how you found the time – with all the things you were constantly doing – to write…or even *read* – all those letters…?

NOËL. Well, don't forget, we weren't twittering and tweeting and emailing and Facebooking…and Linking-In… If we had something to say, we either said it face to face… or we wrote a letter… And I'd like to think some of the things we wrote will still be around when the last email has pressed *delete...*

But one of the most surreal letters I ever received was in 1936 from Greta Garbo – proposing marriage...

GARBO.

"Dear Little Coward,

Received your very loved, small and tiny letter. Dear person, it almost makes me wish the newspapers in this country was right. I am so dreadfully fond of you, that I wish I could forget you. Can't think of anything more terrific than to fall in love with you. Eternally occupied as you are and in need of absolutely no one and looking forward to splendid loneliness completely immune to any female charm! Well, this might be an English lesson.

Anyhow, I take the opportunity to ask if you will be my little bride – (it's leap year, you know). Don't accept, please, I would have to come and get you right away. How you must dislike my writing this way – but – that fluttering, tired and sad heart of mine has been in such a peculiar state since a few weeks ago, but I don't suppose I know you well enough to go into that too much.

I have a very humbling wish that you would write a story for me (us), if you ever have time from the theatre. I can't beg you any harder, as you will do as fits you anyhow – naturally.

Besides that, I would like, horribly I think, to go on dusty roads with you and tell you little fairy tales – beautiful ones about solitary figures living in white castles on top of moonlit mountains (permanent moonlight). And as I finish I must tell you that what I really would like to tell you I haven't told – Darling, you are so flippantly serious."

NOËL. *(Tongue in cheek.)* I very nearly accepted – except that I just knew she'd insist on top billing! But, whatever their foibles, they were all real stars...

Not like a certain famous actress (who shall be nameless) who once explained to me, with perfect seriousness –

ACTRESS. Before making an entrance I always stand aside and let God go on first.

NOËL. I remember that on that particular occasion He gave a singularly uninspired performance. Or the occasion when Lee Strasberg, talking about the legendary Duse...

WOMAN. When she smiled, she didn't merely smile with her mouth but with every part of her body.

NOËL. Which comes under the heading of the neatest trick of the week. Sadly the undoing of so many ladies – the great, the good and the not-so-good, was not an audience, but Anno Domini –

(**MAN** *recites "Epitaph for an Elderly Actress."*)

She got in a rage about age,
And retired in a huff, from the stage
Which taken all round, was a pity,
Because she was still fairly pretty
But she got in a rage about age,
And she moaned and she wept and she wailed,
And she roared and she ranted and railed
And retired, very heavy veiled, from the stage.

MAN. But there *would* be another show. It was called World War II ...There was – it must be admitted – a certain Evelyn Waugh-like quality to the first few months of the war. After all the anticipation – nothing happened. It was called "The Phoney War."

The French called it "*La Guerre Drôle*." But they didn't have very much to laugh about. And not for very long.

WOMAN. Noël was sent to Paris to organize the propaganda "information unit" and wrote the first of what would become a series of verse letters to his secretary, Lorn Loraine, for her to share with Violet and the rest of the Coward family, such as actress Joyce Carey, writer Clemence Dance and his designer, Gladys Calthrop. It was written on British Embassy stationery.

NOËL.

Lornie, whose undying love
Persues me to this foreign clime,
Please note from the address above
That master is not wasting time
In pinching all that he can see
From His Britannic Majesty.

Master regrets he has no news
To gladden Lornie's loving heart
Hitler's still beastly to the Jews
And still the battle does not start.

Kindly inform my aging Mum
That I am reasonably bright
Working for peace and joy to come
By giving dinners every night
Give her my love and also Joyce
Thus echoing your master's voice.

And as for you, my little dear,
Please rest assured of my intense
And most devoted and sincere
And most distinguished compliments
And if you do not care a bit
You know what you can do with it!

Quite early on I realized the job I'd undertaken was neither as important or as serious as I'd been led to believe. Not surprisingly, it was not long before it was – "Adieu, Paris!" and I was sent to America.

WOMAN. But you always had a soft spot for Paris, didn't you?

NOËL. *The last time I saw Paris*
*Her heart was warm and gay**

Yes, Jerry Kern and Oscar Hammerstein knew how much I loved it and dedicated that song to me.

---

*Lines from "The Last Time I Saw Paris" used by permission of Hammerstein Properties LLP.

WOMAN. I was always surprised that *you* never wrote a song about Paris. At one point Cole Porter never seemed to write about anything else.

NOËL. Oh, but I *did* write a Paris song. It was for a musical I started called *Later Than Spring*. I just couldn't make the plot work, so I put it aside and wrote *Sail Away* instead.

I used several of the songs I'd already written but the Paris song didn't quite fit. A pity because I think it had a certain charm...

(**NOËL** *and* **WOMAN** *sing the first and second refrain of* **"I WANTED TO SHOW YOU PARIS."**)

NOËL.

I WANTED TO SHOW YOU PARIS
IN THE SPRING OF THE YEAR,
WHEN ALL THE BLOSSOMS ARE FLAMING, GAILY,
PROCLAIMING, HIGH ROMANCE IS NEAR.
I WANTED TO WALK BESIDE YOU
ON THE BANKS OF THE SEINE
AND TO RECAPTURE THAT BY-GONE DAY
WHEN I FIRST SAW THOSE BARGES DRIFTING BY.
ALONG THE BOULEVARDS AND DOWN THE CHAMPS-
    ÉLYSÉES
THERE'S MUSIC IN THE AIR.
THE LILTING MELODIES OF OFFENBACH AND BIZET
ARE STILL ECHOING THERE.
THIS BEAUTIFUL DAY FOR ME WILL BE FOREVER SUBLIME
IF I CAN SHOW YOU THIS WORLD I KNOW
FOR THE VERY FIRST TIME.

WOMAN.

I WANTED TO SHOW YOU PARIS
IN THE SPRING OF THE YEAR,
FOR WHEN THIS EVER-BEGUILING
CITY IS SMILING,
TROUBLES DISAPPEAR.
I WANTED TO WALK BESIDE YOU
THROUGH THE TREES OF THE BOIS

AND TO REMEMBER THAT DAY THAT ONCE I KNEW
WHEN I WAS GAY AND YOUNG LIKE YOU,
WITH IMPLICATIONS WE'LL REFUSE ALL INVITATIONS
THE WORLD CONSIDERS CHIC.
WE'D RATHER PLAN ON SEEING MANON
AT THE OP'RA COMIQUE THREE TIMES A WEEK.

BOTH.

THIS WONDERFUL DAY FOR ME WILL STAY FOREVER
 SUBLIME
IF YOU WILL SHARE IT MY LOVE WITH ME
FOR THE VERY FIRST TIME.

WOMAN. That's beautiful!

NOËL. I said "Au revoir" so sadly, I just wanted to say "Bonjour encore."

That Paris job during the early part of the war was, frankly, an anticlimax.

As I wrote to a former colleague –

"After all, I'd already been an unofficial spy for several years. Recruited by a senior civil servant at the Foreign Office, who was convinced war was imminent – most of the Government was not. He asked me to go around, as I would anyway, being Noël Coward, singing my little songs and being a bit of a silly ass and then reporting back my impressions of the attitude in the places I had been to.

I thought that being a spy would be more like Mata Hari – and then I told myself... Well, hardly that. I couldn't wear a jewel in my navel, which I believe she was given to doing. Nobody ever issued me with a false beard. In fact the hush-hush side of it was frankly disappointing. Except occasionally I had to look rather idiotic – but that wasn't all that difficult. I'm an *excellent* actor!"

I wasn't the only one frustrated that they weren't allowed to contribute more. My friend, the writer and artist Clemence Dane was another... Frustrated – and yet...as she wrote to me...

CLEMENCE DANE. "I started out doing an occasional morning sitting at a telephone box in a cellar, but no one has ever rung me up! Despairing of that, I've just taken on a temporary weekend job of cooking for policemen.

P.S. Have just come home after frying fifty-three eggs and ten pounds of bacon. I smell to high heaven – and feel much better. Oh how I do love shabby England... I didn't ever before realize quite how much, or how contented the war has made one with what one has."

NOËL. To Aleck Woollcott, a friend since the days of the Algonquin Round Table, I wrote – with America still neutral... "I heard that Ruth Gordon and Helen Hayes among many others have been making strong representations to persuade me to give all this up and return to the theatre! If you should see them at any time, you might explain sweetly and tenderly for me that the reason I cannot at the moment return to the theatre (madly important though I know it to be) is that I am an Englishman and my country is at war! This is a sinister and deadly war, in many ways more so than the last one. There has not been so much bloodshed as yet but, with the kind assistance of press and radio, some very dreadful things are happening to the human spirit. There is no knowing what will survive and what we shall all feel and think. I expect a lot of things will change. I certainly hope so. P.S. I occasionally hurtle up to the front and sing firmly to the troops who are so sunk in mud that they can't escape."

If there were those who kept out of battle, there were many more – like British-born Lynn Fontanne – who yearned to be a part of it and kept the home fires burning...even at a distance.

LYNN. "Darling, darling, we received your lovely letter intact, uncensored, it was wonderful. The first since the dark curtain closed down on us. As you know, we're touring again! And we had a party on the train in the club car, quite unexpected like. It was the day of the

British victory over the *Graf Spee*, it began with Frank
Compton, who was a little, not very tight, suddenly
beginning to sing in a very pleasing voice, "Rule
Britannia," at which, everyone joined in hysterically.
We went from there to the old war songs: "Tipperary,"
"Pack Up Your Troubles," "Keep the Home Fires
Burning." The party ended up with the only German
in the company (whom we strongly suspect of having
pro-Nazi sympathies) standing up with Frank Compton
and me, the only English, and singing with tears rolling
down his cheeks, "God Save the King…"

I feel set apart and with a deeper longing than ever to
come to England, which I feel as if I must never do,
unless I come during the war. Both Alfred and I feel
that we will never be able to look any of you in the eye
unless we do that.

NOËL. Which a little later, they duly did.

Back in London I wrote my impression to Jack Wilson
– my former lover and now my U.S. manager, safely
tucked away in New York… "I honestly can't bear the
thought of leaving England again – except for very
brief periods – till the end of the war. The muddle and
confusion and irritation is almost as bad as ever but the
ordinary people are so magnificent that with all the
discomforts and food rationing and cigarette shortage
and blackouts, I want to be with them.

Travelling in England nowadays is absolute hell and yet
more enjoyable than it ever was before. A few minutes
after you have settled yourself in your first class carriage
it fills up immediately with sailors and soldiers and
wives and children. The trains are mostly all jammed,
there are hardly any porters and you fight your way in
and out of the restaurant car where you are lucky if you
get a very nasty bit of rabbit and some floury potatoes.
But what is so wonderful is that a good time is had by all
and no one is even remotely disagreeable."

WOMAN. Germany surrendered on May 7, 1945, but three days earlier Noël found himself at a dinner party for just four people – one of whom was Winston Churchill. They had had their differences over the years and it was Churchill who had denied Noël the knighthood King George had already approved after Noël made the film, *In Which We Serve* – but all that was in the past.

NOËL. Here was the man who had done more than any other, through this vision, courage and determination to give the Western World one more chance to get things right.

Instinctively, the three of us rose and drank a toast to the old campaigner.

WOMAN. He wrote to Joyce Carey:

NOËL. "Well, Chère, it looks like we've finally got what dear Neville Chamberlain promised us – "Peace in Our Time" – sort of. The only problem is it's nearly a decade and a many thousands of lives later.

So now it's over and I suppose I should share the general jubilation, but somehow I don't. I never for a moment doubted we would win, no matter how black things seemed. We British are at our best in adversity – but we must try and avoid making a habit of it. We won the war but my concern is – how shall we win the *peace?*

Your ever-loving,

Cassandra."

> (**MAN** *sings the third verse of* **"LONDON PRIDE."**)

LONDON PRIDE HAS BEEN HANDED DOWN TO US,
LONDON PRIDE IS A FLOWER THAT'S FREE.
LONDON PRIDE MEANS OUR OWN DEAR TOWN TO US,
AND OUR PRIDE IT FOREVER WILL BE.
GREY CITY,
STUBBORNLY IMPLANTED,
TAKEN SO FOR GRANTED
FOR A THOUSAND YEARS.
STAY, CITY,

SMOKILY ENCHANTED,
CRADLE OF OUR MEMORIES AND OUR HOPES AND FEARS.
EVERY BLITZ,
YOUR RESISTANCE
TOUGHENING.
FROM THE RITZ
TO THE ANCHOR AND CROWN,
NOTHING EVER COULD OVERRIDE
THE PRIDE OF LONDON TOWN.

Well, there are times – and this was certainly one – when you take stock of your life...the places you've seen... the people you've met...some of the things they've said or written to you. There was Virginia Woolf – a rather surprising fan in the 1920's.

WOOLF. "Dear Noël Coward, I am going into the matter of Noël Coward and his plays very seriously. Some of the things in *This Year of Grace* struck me on the forehead like a bullet. And what's more, I remember them and see them enveloped in atmosphere – works of art, in short. I think you ought to bring off something that will put these cautious creeping novels that one has to read silently in an armchair deep, deep in the shade."

NOËL. Well, clearly, I didn't, because our mutual admiration society didn't last – and she never once proposed. But, to counter-balance it, there was a happy rapprochement with another great literary lady – Edith Sitwell.

SITWELL. "I'm having rather a harassing time with lunatics, because I was televised the other day. One wrote to say that I ought to be ashamed of myself, and that I have senile decay and softening of the brain which – oddly enough – makes him respect me. Another has written to me a very long letter about Einstein, telling me I will never get into Space or Time.

A group has seized a poem of mine, 'Still Falls the Rain' – without my permission – and have recited it with their heads out a window. Evidently they don't know it's a poem about the bombing but think it is an advertisement for mackintoshes... Do come round for tea next week.

Your Ancient Friend,

Edith."

NOËL. Edna Ferber – another friend from Round Table days – could write a mean letter and I mean: mean.

FERBER. "The family here tomorrow for Thanksgiving dinner – quaint tribal custom which does not prevail in your land. I have just viewed the uncooked bird – a vast plump white creature that looks appallingly like a decapitated baby."

NOËL. She happened to be staying in Montreux once while I was abroad so she hiked up the mountain to take a look at Chalet Coward.

FERBER. "The house is utterly lovely. It is so livable, so beautiful, so right. The quality that impressed me most was its tranquility. One rarely sees a tranquil dwelling. I may move in, quietly, and barricade the doors and windows against your arrival. That failing, I think you should know that I've enrolled at the Girls' School at Les Avants. I'm taking the courses in Character Crushing and Advanced Curmudgeonry. I'll nip over for tea every afternoon."

NOËL. She was well aware that many people found her negative and acerbic.

FERBER. "Yet I am deeply happy to be alive. I am daily fascinated by existence, when I walk these New York streets. I have a feeling of critically impending doom for our world and this depresses me, not for myself – I've had my life and loved it. Myself, I just want to be put into an old Bergdorf Goodman pasteboard box, such as they use to deliver dresses, and that's that. Don't forget."

NOËL. I used to enjoy trading bons mots – about other people, I might add – with darling Benita Hume.

BENITA. I met Truman Capote once and thought him like a tiny tendril.

NOËL. I met Arlene Francis and thought she was archer than Waterloo Bridge.

BENITA. Margaret Leighton – nice but thin, thin like shredded coconut.

NOËL. I dined with Liz, who was hung with rubies and diamonds and looked like a pregnant pagoda.

BENITA. Elizabeth Taylor's rather voluminous top was secured at such an astonishing height as to give the strong impression that she was wearing epaulettes.

BOTH. I think we could call it a draw...

WOMAN. And of course, Noël had a few subversive male correspondents too. There was Clifton Webb.

NOËL. When he heard of Frank Sinatra's success in a drug drama – *The Man With the Golden Arm* – Clifton wrote: "It is only fair you dash off something for me – *The Man With The Plastic Penis*. It could be sensational, gorgeous and very sincere."

WOMAN. So many letters. A great deal of which were written on his many travels, around the world and back.

NOËL. I have always believed in putting a geographical distance between myself and a flop – whether it was a show or a relationship... I have never liked living anywhere all the year round.

(WOMAN sings "I TRAVEL ALONE.")

WOMAN.

THE WORLD IS WIDE, AND WHEN MY DAY IS DONE
I SHALL AT LEAST HAVE TRAVELLED FREE
LED BY THIS WANDERLUST THAT TURNS MY EYES TO FAR
    HORIZONS.
THOUGH TIME AND TIDE WON'T WAIT FOR ANYONE,
THERE'S ONE ILLUSION LEFT FOR ME
AND THAT'S THE HAPPINESS I'VE KNOWN ALONE.

I TRAVEL ALONE,
SOMETIMES I'M EAST,
SOMETIMES I'M WEST,
NO CHAINS CAN EVER BIND ME;
NO REMEMBERED LOVE CAN EVER FIND ME;

I TRAVEL ALONE
FAIR THOUGH THE FACES AND PLACES I'VE KNOWN,
WHEN THE DREAM IS ENDED AND PASSION HAS FLOWN
I TRAVEL ALONE.
FREE FROM LOVE'S ILLUSION, MY HEART IS MY OWN;
I TRAVEL ALONE.

WOMAN. *(cont.)* Looking back through letters to friends and family over the years, I seem to have had strong opinions on a great variety of places.

WOMAN. He wrote to Cole Lesley:

NOËL. "Dear Coley:

Hong Kong has the most lovely harbor with thousands of ships and sampans and junks farting hither and thither for all the world like tiny insects. And riding along up the hills in chairs. Bumping so much that your teeth rattle and your hat falls off. It's all very slapstick."

"*Marrakech* is not unlike Golders Green. The Moroccans are most sweet but only wish for one thing, which, alas, I am unable to provide. However, affection is what counts."

"In *Jerusalem* there isn't anything to see except places where Jesus *might* have done whatever it was but no one is sure, because, having been razed to the ground eleven times, everything has been built over and over on everything else. And there are far too many churches."

*(*NOËL *sings* "WORLD WEARY.")*

WHEN I'M FEELING DREARY AND BLUE
I'M ONLY TOO
GLAD TO BE LEFT ALONE.
DREAMING OF A PLACE IN THE SUN
WHEN DAY IS DONE,
FAR FROM THE TELEPHONE.
BUSTLE AND THE WEARY CROWD
MAKE ME WANT TO CRY OUT LOUD.
GIVE ME SOMETHING PEACEFUL AND GRAND
WHERE ALL THE LAND
SLUMBERS IN MONOTONE.

I'M WORLD WEARY, WORLD WEARY,
LIVING IN A GREAT BIG TOWN,
I FIND IT SO DREARY, SO DREARY
EVERYTHING LOOKS GREY OR BROWN.
I WANT AN OCEAN BLUE
GREAT BIG TREES
A BIRD'S EYE VIEW
OF THE PYRENEES.

I WANT TO WATCH THE MOON RISE UP
AND SEE THE GREAT RED SUN GO DOWN
WATCHING CLOUDS GO BY
THROUGH A WINTERY SKY
FASCINATES ME
BUT IF I DO IT IN THE STREET,
EVERY COP I MEET
SIMPLY HATES ME,
BECAUSE I'M WORLD WEARY, WORLD WEARY,
I COULD KISS THE RAILROAD TRACKS,
I WANT TO GET RIGHT BACK TO NATURE AND RELAX.

All of which is why I decided to live in Jamaica…

NOËL. *(cont.)* Last night we took a thermos full of cocktails up and sat and watched the sun set and the lights come up over the town and it really was magical. The sky changed from deep blue to yellow and pale green and then all the color went and out came the stars and the fireflies. The view is really staggering, particularly when the light begins to go and the far mountains become purple against a pale lemon sky.

There is a very sweet white owl who comes and hoots at us every evening. I don't think he does it in any spirit of criticism but just to be friendly. When it decides to rain here there are no half measures about it. It comes down in a deluge and there is already some valuable Penicillin growing in all my shoes!

And, of course, being British, the plumbing came as no surprise to me… Mine proved to be a trifle eccentric. My lavatory has hiccups and sprays my behind with cold water every now and then, which is all very gay and sanitary. The biggest hurricane since Tallulah Bankhead has just avoided the island. We had a dear little earthquake on Saturday morning. I was on the loo at the time and put the strange rumbling to natural causes.

NOËL. *(cont.)*That apart, I loved every moment of it!

WOMAN. Of course, there were the visitors. They *all* came...

NOËL. Some more welcome than others... "Oh, we must drop in on dear old Noëlie!" Being British, of course, one took the rough with the smooth – and sometimes even with the rough. But without a doubt, our star guest was the darling Queen Mum.

She told her "minders"...

QUEEN MUM. "You can mind your P's as well as your Q's and, no matter *what* the itinerary says, I am jolly well going to have lunch with my friend, Noël Coward."

NOËL. And, indeed, she did – a wonderful two hour feet up with just us – me, Alfred and Lynn.

In the end it was all about people, really. Not the places. Not even the plays. But the people. So many of them. They've all gone now, of course.

Time's wingèd chariot and ever-rolling stream and all that. But we did have a lot of laughs – and a few tears.

WOMAN. In his last TV interview Noël was asked to sum up his life in one word.

He paused uncharacteristically, then said...

"Now comes the terrible decision as to whether to be corny or not.

There *is* one word. *Love.* To know that you are among people you love and who love you. That has made all the successes wonderful – much more wonderful than they'd have been anyway.

And that's it, really. That's it."

> (**NOËL** *sings the poem,* "*When I Have Fears,*" *unaccompanied. The melody should be improvised.*)

NOËL.

    WHEN I FEEL SAD, AS KEATS FELT SAD,
    THAT MY LIFE IS SO NEARLY DONE
    IT GIVES ME COMFORT TO DWELL UPON
    REMEMBERED FRIENDS WHO ARE DEAD AND GONE
    AND THE JOKES WE HAD AND THE FUN
    HOW HAPPY THEY ARE I CANNOT KNOW
    BUT HAPPY AM I WHO LOVED THEM SO.

WOMAN. He always said he didn't mind where it all ended –

NOËL. – Just that I would prefer Fate to allow me to go to sleep when it was my proper bedtime. I never have been one for staying up too late.

WOMAN. And Fate did just that. It had been a *marvellous* party.

MAN. I couldn't have liked it more!

    *(***MAN*** and ***WOMAN*** sing the refrain of **"THE PARTY'S OVER NOW."***)*

WOMAN.

    THE PARTY'S OVER NOW,
    THE DAWN IS DRAWING VERY NIGH
    THE CANDLES GUTTER,
    THE STARLIGHT LEAVES THE SKY.

MAN.

    IT'S TIME FOR LITTLE BOYS AND GIRLS
    TO HURRY HOME TO BED,
    FOR THERE'S A NEW DAY
    WAITING JUST AHEAD.

BOTH.

    LIFE IS SWEET,
    BUT TIME IS FLEET
    BENEATH THE MAGIC OF THE MOON.
    DANCING TIME
    MAY SEEM SUBLIME

MAN.

    BUT IT IS ENDED ALL TOO SOON.

BOTH.
> THE THRILL HAS GONE,
> TO LINGER ON
> WOULD SPOIL IT ANYHOW;
> LET'S CREEP AWAY FROM THE DAY,
> FOR THE PARTY'S OVER NOW.

The End

*(Encore song: **"I'LL SEE YOU AGAIN."**)*

BOTH.

I'LL SEE YOU AGAIN
WHENEVER SPRING BREAKS THROUGH AGAIN.
TIME MAY LIE HEAVY BETWEEN,
BUT WHAT HAS BEEN,
IS PAST FORGETTING.
YOUR SWEET MEMORY
ACROSS THE YEARS WILL COME TO ME;
THOUGH MY WORLD MAY GO AWRY,
IN MY HEART 'TWILL EVER LIE,
JUST THE ECHO OF A SIGH,
GOODBYE.

APPENDIX

Past productions of *Love, Noël* included different lyrics and musical arrangements for a number of songs in the current script and score. Interested licensees are allowed to use the proceeding alternate lyrics for their performances. Use of these alternate versions will require further musical preparation from music directors. Samuel French, Inc. does not provide further music arrangements for these versions.

Page 15: *"MAD ABOUT THE BOY"*

GERTIE.

> MAD ABOUT THE BOY,
> IT'S PRETTY FUNNY BUT I'M MAD ABOUT THE BOY.
> HE HAS A STRANGE APPEAL
> THAT MAKES ME FEEL
> THERE'S MAYBE SOMETHING SAD ABOUT THE BOY.
> WALKING DOWN THE STREET
> HIS EYES LOOK OUT AT ME FROM PEOPLE THAT I MEET.
> I CAN'T BELIEVE IT'S TRUE
> BUT WHEN I'M BLUE
> IN SOME STRANGE WAY I'M GLAD ABOUT THE BOY.
> LORD KNOWS I'M NOT A FOOL GIRL,
> I REALLY SHOULDN'T CARE.
> LORD KNOWS I'M NOT A SCHOOLGIRL
> IN THE FLURRY OF HER FIRST AFFAIR.
> WILL IT EVER CLOY?
> THIS ODD DIVERSITY OF MISERY AND JOY?
> THIS DREAM THAT PAINS ME
> AND ENCHAINS ME,
> BUT I CAN'T BECAUSE I'M MAD ABOUT THE BOY!

Page 27: *"WHY DO THE WRONG PEOPLE TRAVEL?"*

NOËL.

> WHY DO THE WRONG PEOPLE TRAVEL, TRAVEL, TRAVEL,
> WHEN THE RIGHT PEOPLE STAY BACK HOME?
> WHAT COMPULSION COMPELS THEM

AND WHO THE HELL TELLS THEM
TO DRAG THEIR CANS TO ZANZIBAR,
INSTEAD OF STAYING QUIETLY IN OMAHA?
THE TAJ MAHAL
AND THE GRAND CANAL
AND THE SUNNY FRENCH RIVIERA
WOULD BE LESS OPPRESSED
IF THE MIDDLE WEST
WOULD SETTLE FOR SOMEWHERE RATHER NEARER.
PLEASE DO NOT THINK THAT I CRITICIZE OR CAVIL
AT A GENUINE URGE TO ROAM
BUT WHY, OH WHY, DO THE WRONG PEOPLE TRAVEL
WHEN THE RIGHT PEOPLE STAY BACK HOME,
I'M MERELY ASKING
WHY THE RIGHT PEOPLE STAY BACK HOME?

WHY DO THE WRONG PEOPLE TRAVEL, TRAVEL, TRAVEL,
WHEN THE RIGHT PEOPLE STAY BACK HOME?
WHAT EXPLAINS THIS MASS MANIA
TO LEAVE PENNSYLVANIA
AND CLACK AROUND LIKE FLOCKS OF GEESE,
DEMANDING DRY MARTINIS ON THE ISLES OF GREECE?
MILLIONS OF TOURISTS ARE CHURNING UP THE GRAVEL
WHILE THEY GAZE AT ST. PETER'S DOME,
BUT WHY OH WHY DO THE WRONG PEOPLE TRAVEL
WHEN THE RIGHT PEOPLE STAY BACK HOME?
I SOMETIMES WONDER
WHY THE RIGHT PEOPLE STAY BACK HOME.

WHY DO THE WRONG PEOPLE TRAVEL, TRAVEL,
WHEN THE RIGHT PEOPLE STAY BACK HOME?
WHAT PECULIAR OBSESSIONS
INSPIRE THOSE PROCESSIONS
OF FAMILIES FROM HOUSTON, TEX,
WITH ALL THOSE CAMERAS AROUND THEIR NECKS?
THEY WILL TAKE A TRAIN
OR AN AEROPLANE
FOR AN HOUR ON THE COSTA BRAVA,
AND THEY'LL SEE POMPEII
ON THE ONLY DAY

THAT IT'S UP TO ITS ASS IN MOLTEN LAVA.
IT WOULD TAKE YEARS TO UNRAVEL – RAVEL – RAVEL
EVERY IMPULSE THAT MAKES THEM ROAM,
BUT WHY OH WHY DO THE WRONG PEOPLE TRAVEL
WHEN THE RIGHT PEOPLE STAY BACK HOME?
WON'T SOMEONE TELL ME
WHY THE RIGHT PEOPLE STAY BACK HOME?

Page 31: *"NEVER AGAIN"*

WOMAN.

NO, NEVER AGAIN,
NEVER THE STRANGE UNTHINKING JOY,
NEVER THE PAIN,
LET ME BE WISE,
LET ME LEARN TO DOUBT ROMANCE,
TRY TO LIVE WITHOUT ROMANCE,
LET ME BE SANE.
TIME CHANGES THE TUNE
CHANGES THE PALE UNWINKING STARS,
EVEN THE MOON.
LET ME BE SOON
STRONG ENOUGH TO FLOUT ROMANCE –
AND SAY, "YOU'RE OUT, ROMANCE,"
NEVER AGAIN.

(Firmly.)

NEVER AGAIN.

(Pause.)

NEVER.

(Questioningly.)

NEVER?
AGAIN?

Page 32: *"BRONXVILLE DARBY AND JOAN"*
BOTH.

WE DO NOT FEAR THE VERDICT OF POSTERITY
OUR LIVES HAVE BEEN TOO HUMDRUM AND MUNDANE

WOMAN.

IN THE TWILIGHT OF OUR DAYS

MAN.

HAVING REACHED THE FINAL PHASE

WOMAN.

IN ALL SINCERITY

MAN.

WE MUST EXPLAIN:

BOTH.

WE'RE A DEAR OLD COUPLE AND WE HATE ONE ANOTHER
AND WE'VE HATED ONE ANOTHER FOR A LONG, LONG
TIME.

MAN.

SINCE THE DAY WE WERE WED, UP TO THE PRESENT,
OUR LIVES, WE MUST CONFESS
HAVE BEEN PROGRESSIVELY MORE UNPLEASANT.

BOTH.

WE'RE JUST SWEET OLD DARLINGS WHO DESPISE ONE
ANOTHER
WITH A THOROUGHNESS APPROACHING THE SUBLIME,
BUT THROUGH ALL OUR YEARS
WE'VE BEEN AFFECTIONATELY KNOWN
AS THE BRONXVILLE DARBY AND JOAN.

MAN.

OUR GOLDEN WEDDING PASSED WITH ALL OUR FAMILY

WOMAN.

AN ORGY OF REMEMBRANCE AND RUE,

MAN.

IN ACKNOWLEDGEMENT OF THIS

WOMAN.

WE EXCHANGED A LOVING KISS
A TRIFLE CLAMMILY

BOTH.

BECAUSE WE KNEW:
WE'RE A DEAR OLD COUPLE WHO DETEST ONE ANOTHER,
WE'VE DETESTED ONE ANOTHER SINCE OUR BRIDAL NIGHT,
WHICH WAS SQUALID, UNATTRACTIVE AND CONVULSIVE

AND PROVED, BEYOND DISPUTE,
THAT WE WERE MUTUALLY REPULSIVE.
WE'RE JUST SWEET OLD DARLINGS
WHO TORMENT ONE ANOTHER
WITH THE UTMOST MALICIOUSNESS AND SPITE,
AND THROUGH ALL OUR YEARS
WE'VE BEEN INACCURATELY KNOWN
AS THE BRONXVILLE DARBY AND JOAN.

WE'RE A DEAR OLD COUPLE AND WE LOATHE ONE
ANOTHER
WITH A LOATHING THAT ENGULFS US LIKE A TIDAL WAVE,

WOMAN.

WITH OUR DEEP SUB-CONSCIOUS MINDS WE SELDOM
DABBLE
BUT SOMETHING MUST IMPEL
THE WORDS WE SPELL
WHEN WE'RE PLAYING SCRABBLE.

MAN.

WE'RE JUST SWEET OLD DARLINGS WHO ABHOR ONE
ANOTHER

WOMAN.

AND WE'LL BORE EACH OTHER FIRMLY TO THE GRAVE

BOTH.

BUT THROUGH ALL OUR YEARS WE'VE BEEN REFERRED TO
MORE OR LESS
AS THE BRONXVILLE PORGY AND BESS.

Page 40: *"I WANTED TO SHOW YOU PARIS"*

MAN.

I WANTED TO SHOW YOU PARIS
IN THE SPRING OF THE YEAR,
WHEN ALL THE BLOSSOMS ARE FLAMING, GAILY,
PROCLAIMING, HIGH ROMANCE IS NEAR.
I WANTED TO WALK BESIDE YOU
ON THE BANKS OF THE SEINE
AND TO RECAPTURE THAT BY-GONE DAY
WHEN I FIRST SAW THOSE BARGES DRIFTING BY.

ALONG THE BOULEVARDS AND DOWN THE CHAMPS-
    ÉLYSÉES
THERE'S MUSIC IN THE AIR.
THE LILTING MELODIES OF OFFENBACH AND BIZET
ARE STILL ECHOING THERE.
THIS BEAUTIFUL DAY FOR ME WILL BE FOREVER SUBLIME
IF I CAN SHOW YOU THIS WORLD I KNOW
FOR THE VERY FIRST TIME.

WOMAN.

HOW LOVELY TO BE IN PARIS
IN THE SPRING OF THE YEAR,
FOR EVEN WHEN THIS EVER-BEGUILING
CITY IS SMILING,
TROUBLES DISAPPEAR.
HOW LOVELY TO WATCH THE DANCING WORLD
GO HURRYING BY
AND TO REMEMBER THIS WARM ENCHANTED GLOW,
STARS ABOVE AND LIGHTS BELOW.
ALTHOUGH I CAN'T UNDERSTAND
A WORD THEY'RE SAYING, UNTIL MY DYING DAY
I'LL CALL TO MIND THE KIND
OF MUSIC THEY ARE PLAYING
AND FEEL SUDDENLY GAY.

BOTH.

THIS WONDERFUL DAY FOR ME
WILL STAY FOREVER SUBLIME,
BECAUSE I'M FEELING
THAT LIFE'S WORTHWHILE
FOR THE VERY FIRST TIME.

Page 48: *"WORLD WEARY"*

MAN.

WHEN I'M FEELING DREARY AND BLUE
I'M ONLY TOO
GLAD TO BE LEFT ALONE.
DREAMING OF A PLACE IN THE SUN
WHEN DAY IS DONE,
FAR FROM THE TELEPHONE.

BUSTLE AND THE WEARY CROWD
MAKE ME WANT TO CRY OUT LOUD.
GIVE ME SOMETHING PEACEFUL AND GRAND
WHERE ALL THE LAND
SLUMBERS IN MONOTONE.

I'M WORLD WEARY, WORLD WEARY,
LIVING IN A GREAT BIG TOWN,
I FIND IT SO DREARY, SO DREARY
EVERYTHING LOOKS GREY OR BROWN.
I WANT AN OCEAN BLUE
GREAT BIG TREES
A BIRD'S EYE VIEW
OF THE PYRENEES.

I WANT TO WATCH THE MOON RISE UP
AND SEE THE GREAT RED SUN GO DOWN
WATCHING CLOUDS GO BY
THROUGH A WINTERY SKY
FASCINATES ME
BUT IF I DO IT IN THE STREET,
EVERY COP I MEET
SIMPLY HATES ME,
BECAUSE I'M WORLD WEARY, WORLD WEARY,
I COULD KISS THE RAILROAD TRACKS,
I WANT TO GET RIGHT BACK TO NATURE AND RELAX.

I'M WORLD WEARY, WORLD WEARY
TIRED OF ALL THOSE JUMPING JACKS!
I WANT TO GET RIGHT BACK TO NATURE AND RELAX.